Also by Doreen Cronin

Bounce
Click, Clack, Boo!
Click, Clack, Moo: Cows That Type
Click, Clack, Quackity-Quack
Click, Clack, Splish, Splash
Dooby Dooby Moo
Duck for President
Giggle, Giggle, Quack,
M.O.M. (Mom Operating Manual)
Stretch
Thump, Quack, Moo
Wiggle

Doreen Cronin

Illustrated by Kevin Cornell

A Atheneum Books for Young Readers

atheneum New York   London   Toronto   Sydney   New Delhi

ATHENEUM BOOKS FOR YOUNG READERS

An imprint of Simon & Schuster Children's Publishing Division

1230 Avenue of the Americas, New York, New York 10020

This book is a work of fiction. Any references to historical events, real people, or real places are used fictitiously. Other names, characters, places, and events are products of the author's imagination, and any resemblance to actual events or places or persons, living or dead, is entirely coincidental.

Text copyright © 2014 by Doreen Cronin

Illustrations copyright © 2014 by Kevin Cornell

All rights reserved, including the right of reproduction in whole or in part in any form.

ATHENEUM BOOKS FOR YOUNG READERS is a registered trademark of Simon & Schuster, Inc.

Atheneum logo is a trademark of Simon & Schuster, Inc.

For information about special discounts for bulk purchases, please contact Simon & Schuster Special Sales at 1-866-506-1949 or business@simonandschuster.com.

The Simon & Schuster Speakers Bureau can bring authors to your live event. For more information or to book an event, contact the Simon & Schuster Speakers Bureau at 1-866-248-3049 or visit our website at www.simonspeakers.com.

Book design by Sonia Chaghatzbanian

The text for this book is set in Garth Graphic.

The illustrations for this book are rendered in graphite, watercolor, and digital.

Manufactured in the United States of America

1114 FFG

10 9 8 7 6 5 4 3

CIP data for this book is available from the Library of Congress.

ISBN 978-1-4424-9676-7

ISBN 978-1-4424-9678-1 (eBook)

For Poppy and Sweetie, of course!
—D. C.

To Kim, who holds my hand
—K. C.

Introductions

Welcome to the yard!

Meet the Chicken Squad: Four fuzzy little chicks who should fill their days pecking chicken feed and chasing bugs but instead spend most of their time looking for trouble and finding it. My job is to pull them out of it. My name's J. J. Tully, retired search-and-rescue dog. Seven years on the job, two years in the yard. Keep your eye on these four:

Dirt: Short, yellow, fuzzy

Real Name: Peep

Specialty: Foreign languages, math, colors, computer codes

Sugar: Short, yellow, fuzzy

Real Name: Little Boo

Specialty: Breaking and entering, interrupting

Poppy: Short, yellow, fuzzy

Real Name: Poppy

Specialty: Watching the shoe (will explain later)

Sweetie: Short, yellow, fuzzy

Real Name: Sweet Coconut Louise

Specialty: None that I can see

Here's the thing: I can't watch them all the time. I have dog stuff to do. Keep your eyes on them for a while, will you? I'm just going to settle down and take a little nap. Wake me if they get into any trouble. Well, *big* trouble. I'm sure you can handle a *little* trouble on your own.

Chapter 1

Help!! Help!"

A squirrel came barreling into the chicken coop. He was out of breath and in a panic. "There is something big and scary in the yard!" gasped the squirrel. "It's after me!"

"Describe it for me," said Sugar. She pulled her notepad out of the old shoe.

"It's big and scary!!" said the squirrel. "It's BIG and it's SCARY!!"

"Big and scary is not going to cut it," said Sugar. "Lots of things are big and

scary, kid. My mom is big and scary. Try again."

"It's ENORMOUS and FRIGHTEN-ING," said Squirrel.

Sugar put her pencil down. "Better. Keep going."

"It's HUGE and TERRIFYING!" cried the squirrel.

"Much better, Tail," said Sugar. She checked her notes.

Big and Scary!
Enormous and Frightening!
Huge and Terrifying!

"Maybe I can help," said Dirt. She took out her sketchpad. "What shape was it?" asked Dirt.

"It was . . . big," answered the squirrel.

"*Big* is not a shape," sighed Sugar. She put her notebook down. "You've got a good vocabulary, kid. But your poor shape knowledge means I can't respect you. You should go now."

"Hold on, Sugar,"

said Dirt. "Let's figure this out. Let's start from the beginning."

"It's *ENORMOUS*!" snapped the squirrel. He was starting to get grumpy.

"I thought you said it was *big*," said Sugar.

"Maybe I can give it a try," said Dirt. "Is it bigger than a house?"

"Well, no," said the squirrel.

"Is it bigger than the chicken coop?" asked Dirt.

"Well, no," answered the squirrel.

"Is it bigger than you?" asked Dirt.

"I am a brave squirrel!! Of course it's bigger than me!" said the squirrel. "Why would I be afraid of something if it wasn't bigger than me?"

"Lots of people are afraid of things that are smaller than they are," said Dirt.

"Well, not me," said the squirrel. "I'm only afraid of one thing and it's

BIG and **SCARY**, and it came out of nowhere, and it's out there waiting for me!"

"I think we need J. J. on this case," said Sugar. "He knows the yard like the back of his paw. I'm going to run over there and ask him to join us."

"Not the dog!" yelled the squirrel. "Not the DOG! NOT THE DOG!"

"What's your beef with the dog, Tail?" asked Sugar.

"He's *big* and *scary*!" answered the squirrel.

Sugar had a hunch.

"Fine, I'm just going to run outside and grab a shovel," she announced. "I'll be right back."

"Not the shovel!" said Tail. "Not the SHOVEL! NOT THE SHOVEL!"

"What's your beef with the shovel?" asked Sugar.

"It's big and scary!" said the squirrel.

"I give up, Tail," said Sugar. "Sounds to me like you're afraid of *everything* in the yard. Now get out of here and call me when you have a real problem." Sugar made a last note on her pad.

Big and Scary!
Enormous and Frightening!
Huge and Terrifying!
Never mind!

Just then a dark figure appeared in the doorway and cast a shadow over Dirt, Sugar, and Tail.

Chapter 2

How was I supposed to know the twitchy squirrel was going to faint? I mean, sure, sometimes I chase him around the yard. Big deal. You'd do the same thing if you were a dog. Especially if you were bored out of your mind and had nothing to read. So yeah, the squirrel took one look at my mug and fainted.

Like I mentioned, it's my job to keep the Chicken Squad and their mom, Moosh, safe and sound. I saw the squirrel walking into the chicken coop that afternoon, and I wouldn't be doing my job if I didn't check it out. Moosh saw it too. She wouldn't be doing her job if she didn't check it out either. But Moosh and I have both been around long enough to know that squirrels are never up to anything good.

"Now look what you did, J. J.," said Sugar, frowning at the squirrel stretched out on the floor. She did not look pleased.

Poppy and Sweetie jumped out of the shoe to get a closer look.

"It's so soft!" said Sweetie. "Can we keep it?"

"Dead squirrels are boring," said Poppy. "I'll be in the shoe if you need me."

Moosh burst into the coop, looked down at the squirrel, and rolled her eyes.

"I'll handle it," she said.

So there was only one thing left for me to do: go back to sleep.

Chapter 3

I hope that's not what I think it is," said Moosh.

"What do you think it is?" asked Dirt.

"A dead squirrel in my living room," she answered.

"The squirrel's not dead, Mom," said Sugar. "He just fainted."

"How can you be so sure?" asked Moosh. "He looks dead to me."

"Dead things smell bad," answered Sugar. "He just smells like squirrel."

Moosh stepped right over the squirrel and walked to the old shoe. She plucked out Poppy by the scruff of his neck and then dropped him on the floor. "*You* are starting to smell like dirty feet," she said. "Time for a bath." Then she asked Sugar and Dirt, "What's he doing here, anyway?"

"He claims there's something big and scary in the yard," said Sugar.

"Typical squirrel," said Moosh.

The squirrel started to moan and twitch.

"Sounds like he's coming around," said Moosh out of the side of her beak. "Drag him outside. He smells bad."

Chapter 4

You are one delicate squirrel," Sugar remarked. Tail was awake, but his eyes were wide, and his color was not good.

"What would you call that particular shade of gray, Dirt?" asked Sugar.

"We've got more important things to do here, Sugar," said Dirt. She studied the squirrel.

"No, we don't," said Sugar.

"You're probably right." Dirt put her sketchpad down and took out her big box of crayons. "It's a cross between timberwolf gray and manatee gray. It's definitely not regular gray. More like I-think-I-may-pass-out-again gray."

"Why don't we call it 'Scaredy Squirrel Gray'?" said Sugar.

"I like it," said Dirt.

"Perfect," said Sugar. "Now, let's get back to business."

"Is the dog gone?" asked Tail. His whole body twitched. "Is the dog GONE? IS THE DOG GONE?"

"Listen, kid," said Sugar. "J. J. doesn't want to catch you. He is never going to catch you. If he wanted to catch you, he would have caught you already and tossed you over the fence, like an old sock. He just chases you for fun."

"I don't believe you," said Tail.

"Suit yourself," said Sugar. "No skin off my teeth if you spend the rest of your life looking over your shoulder."

"Was the big and scary thing a *rhombus*?" asked Dirt. Her sketchpad was in her hands again.

"Tail here doesn't know a circle from a triangle, and you're going to start with a rhombus?"

"Do *you* know what a rhombus is, Sugar?" asked Dirt.

"No," said Sugar. "And I don't want to know."

"A rhombus looks like this." Dirt drew a diamond on her sketchpad.

"I am a brave squirrel," Tail repeated. "Brave squirrels are not afraid of diamonds!"

"Okaaaay," said Dirt. "How about a

triangle?" She did a quick sketch and showed it to Tail.

"Could be," said Tail. "Maybe. I'm not sure."

"Follow me, kid," said Sugar, walking back to the coop.

"Hey, Sweetie," called Sugar. "Come on out here."

Sweetie popped her head out of the shoe. She was eating a carrot.

"Did the big and scary thing look like that?" asked Sugar.

"Big and scary things are not shaped like carrots!" said Tail.

"Not the carrot, kid," said Sugar. "Sweetie's got a weird triangle head. Did it look like that?"

"No, definitely not," said the squirrel.

"This is going to take all day," said Sugar. "Maybe Tail here can go to squirrel kindergarten, learn some shapes, and then get back to us. Don't we have anything better to do?"

"Not really," answered Dirt. She drew something else. "How about this?"

The squirrel tried to scream, but

fainted before he got it out of his mouth.

"Nice work, Dirt," said Sugar.

"So, the big and scary thing in the yard is a circle," said Dirt, tapping her sketchpad with her pencil. "Interesting."

"So Tail is either afraid of the birdbath or the blow-up pool," announced Sugar. She looked down at her notes:

Nervous squirrel with good vocabulary and poor shape skills is terrified of something round in the yard.

Also, Dirt discovers a new shade of gray.

"Can we please do something about the dead squirrel in the living room??" asked Moosh. She deposited a clean-smelling Poppy just inside the

chicken coop and then headed back out the door. "If it's still here when I get back from my gardening, I'm going to make a rug out of it."

Chapter 5

"Listen, Tail," said Sugar. She was standing on the squirrel's neck. "My mom says that if you are still dead when she gets back, she's going to use you as a carpet. So if you want help, you need to face your fear of shapes like a big boy."

"Ow, my head," said Tail. "Let me

up. I am a brave squirrel. No more fainting, I promise. It was just so . . . so . . ."

"*Big* and *scary*," said Sugar. "We get it."

"You did great, Tail," said Dirt. "Now we know the big, scary thing is in the shape of a circle."

"Yes! A circle! A big circle," said Tail. "A really big, shiny circle. It came out of nowhere and then stopped approximately four feet off the ground. It was a dark shade of green. Not quite forest green, but close. Possibly hunter green. After a while it made a weird hissing and popping noise. And it interrupted the atmosphere."

"That's quite an improvement over 'big and scary,'" said Sugar. "You ought to bump your head more often, kid."

"I don't think I like you," said Tail.

"I'm okay with that," said Sugar.

"What do you mean, 'interrupted

the atmosphere'?" asked Dirt. Sugar was paying close attention while she wrote in her pad.

"Good question," said Sugar.

"Thank you," said Dirt.

"First it lit up," said the squirrel. "Then I saw a giant door close. I ran away for a while and when I came back, the air around it looked really weird."

"Interesting," said Sugar, scribbling down notes.

Dirt was drawing as fast as she could. She put her crayons down and gasped. Sugar looked at the drawing and then looked at her own notes:

Round
Shiny
Atmospheric Disturbance
   (aka weird air)
Gasp!

"Gasp!" said Sugar.

"Gasp!" said Dirt.

Sugar took a deep breath and then slowly exhaled.

"You've got a big problem, Tail."

"What is it? What is it? What is it?"

"This is a HUGE problem."

"What? What? What?"

"Kid, you have one ENORMOUS problem!"

"WHAT??????"

"You've got a UFO on your tail, Tail. An unidentified flying object. And I suspect it's not leaving until you get in it and fly away."

The squirrel started to turn that weird shade of gray again.

"Don't do it, Tail," said Sugar. "You hit the floor one more time, and my mom's going to put you under the coffee table."

"A UFO?" the squirrel squawked. "What would a UFO want with a squirrel?

"Maybe they want you for a pet," Sugar suggested.

"Squirrels make terrible pets!" said Poppy.

"You took the words right out of my mouth," said Sugar.

Chapter 6

Poppy dropped his carrot and cried out. "Mom is in the yard! We have to go get her before the aliens grab her."

"Don't get your feathers in a bunch, Poppy," said Sugar. "UFOs don't want chickens."

"Why not?" asked Poppy. "Chickens are way better than squirrels!"

"Are not!" said Tail.

"Are too!" said Poppy.

"Are not!" said Tail.

"Are too!" said Poppy.

"Let me handle this," said Sugar. "You know that nice lady Barbara, who lives in the main house?" Squirrel nodded. "Did Barbara build you a house to keep you warm and snug?"

"Well, no."

"Does Barbara come out here every day just to feed you?" asked Sugar.

"No."

"Did Barbara get a dog just to keep you safe?" asked Sugar.

"No."

"I'm on to something here," said Sugar. "Chickens are unique, beautiful, talented, special, and extraordinarily rare. But squirrels . . . are none of those things. . . ."

"HEY! I resent that!" said Tail.

"Let me finish, Tail," said Sugar.

"Squirrels are everywhere. Gray ones, black ones, big ones, fat ones. They are common, ordinary, boring creatures." Sugar went to the door and looked out into the yard.

"I'm not sure I follow you, Sugar," said Dirt.

"My point is that no self-respecting alien in his or her right mind is going to bring back a common, ordinary, boring creature as a pet."

"I am definitely not following you," said Sweetie.

"I'm saying the UFO isn't here for you, Tail," said Sugar slowly. "That UFO is here . . . for us."

"Us?" Now it was Sweetie's turn to drop a carrot.

"The aliens have come for chickens," Sugar said decisively. "I always knew this would happen one day."

"You did?" asked Sweetie.

"Mom is out there!!" cried Poppy for the second time.

"I don't see her anywhere," said Sugar, looking out into the yard. "Quick. We have to act fast! Poppy, Sweetie, go to the supply room and get me grass clippings, a bag of rocks, a ball of string, a tank of helium, and an orange balloon."

"Chickens couldn't possibly have all those things!" said the squirrel.

"Then you don't know chickens, Tail," said Sugar. "You don't know chickens at all."

Chapter 7

Sugar and Dirt were packing up their equipment so they could rescue Moosh from the UFO. Poppy lugged a bag full of rocks, and Sweetie carried a box of grass clippings, a tank of helium, and an orange balloon.

"You can't leave me here alone!" cried the squirrel. "You CAN'T! YOU

CAN'T!!" Squirrel threw himself onto the floor and grabbed Sugar's tiny leg.

Sugar shook him off.

"How did you do that?" asked Dirt.

"My legs are too skinny to get a good grip," answered Sugar. She turned to the squirrel. "You're coming with us, Tail. But you have to keep quiet. And quit twitching. It attracts attention, and it makes me nervous."

"I'm *not* going back out there," cried the squirrel. "Never. Never. NEVER!"

"Listen, Tail," said Sugar. "You're going to do exactly what I tell you to do. There are aliens out there. Aliens looking for chickens. My mother is out

there. My mother is a chicken. Do you follow me?"

The room fell quiet.

The squirrel's eyes got wide again.

"Don't even think about fainting, kid," said Sugar. "I'll drag you out there myself and toss you into that UFO. I'm pretty sure they'll toss you back. But I'm willing to take that risk."

"You are a brave squirrel," said Dirt. "Be brave."

"What do we do with the grass clippings?" asked Poppy.

"Camouflage," said Sugar. "Poppy, you lick Sweetie. Sweetie, you lick Poppy. Then roll around in the grass clippings. You'll be camouflaged. When you're done, lick Dirt and do the same."

"I will not be licked by a chicken!" announced the squirrel.

"Trust me," said Sugar, "I would never ask anyone in my family to lick a squirrel. You're on your own, pal."

Poppy and Sweetie followed Sugar's instructions to lick and roll. Sweetie rolled right out the door. Poppy rolled her back. When they all looked like stubby clumps of grass, Sugar said, "Now grab the rocks and head to the tomato patch. On my signal, you let loose."

"Got it!" said Poppy. "But who's going to watch the shoe?"

"Forget the shoe," said Sugar. "Dirt, you take the helium and stick with Tail. He's going to show you where the UFO landed. Send up the balloon when you get there. That's our target, everyone!"

"Got it," answered Dirt. "What are you going to do, Sugar?"

"I'd rather not say," answered Sugar, lowering her voice. "It's dangerous, and I don't want to frighten the squirrel."

"You're right," agreed Dirt. "The less information he has, the better."

"Move out!" said Sugar.

"Wait," said the squirrel. "Wouldn't it be easier to just blow up the balloon here instead of dragging a helium tank all way across the yard?"

Sugar let out a heavy sigh.

"You can't camouflage yourself and then walk around with a giant, orange balloon!" snapped Sugar. "Think, squirrel, think!"

"Wow," said the squirrel. "You guys are good."

Chapter 8

Tail led the way with Dirt right behind him. When they got closer to the back of the house, he stopped cold.

"There it is," whispered the squirrel. He pressed his body against the house. "There it IS! THERE IT IS!"

Dirt stepped in front of the squirrel

and placed her wing to her lips. Then she peeked around the side. She gasped. Sure enough, a few feet from the house, was a giant circle, about four feet off the ground. She had never seen it before.

"That *is* big and scary. You were right," said Dirt. "And that is definitely a circle. Nice work!" Dirt studied the giant circle for another minute. "Although that is absolutely not forest green. Or pine green. That is clearly asparagus green. Don't you own a box of crayons?"

Tail's eyes were wide. "What now?" he asked.

"We get down low and we crawl,"
said Dirt. "They'll never see us."

"I'm big and gray! They'll see me,"

cried the squirrel. "They'll see ME! THEY'LL SEE ME!"

"They don't *want* you," Dirt reminded him. "Just do as I say and everything will be fine."

Tail started to turn Scaredy Squirrel Gray again.

"Repeat after me," said Dirt. "I am a brave squirrel."

"I am a brave squirrel. I am a BRAVE squirrel. I AM A BRAVE SQUIRREL!" The color returned to his face.

They crawled closer to the UFO. It was hissing and popping. The air around it made everything look wavy.

"Now what?" asked the squirrel.

"We blow up the balloon," answered Dirt, "and we tie it to that flowerpot next to the UFO."

"Then what?" asked the squirrel.

"We wait for the others," said Dirt calmly.

"What are they going to do?" asked the squirrel.

"I never know, kid," answered Dirt. "I never, ever know."

Chapter 9

Doink

Doink, doink.

Doink, doink, doink, doink.

It sounded like stones bouncing off something metal. I jumped up from my nap and ran outside.

That's when I saw Barbara's brand-new, shiny, green barbecue being pelted by rocks. Dozens of them. They were coming from the tomato patch.

Doink doink doinkdoinkdoinkdoink doinkdoinkdoinkdoink doinkdoinkdoink-doink doinkdoinkdoinkdoink.

I ran as fast as I could toward the patch and took a couple of hits myself. That's where I found two clumps of

grass hurling pebbles at the back deck.

"What are you doing?" I yelled. I grabbed the bag of rocks with my teeth and dragged it away from them. And then I tripped—over an old, green shoe.

"Calm down! What on Earth is wrong with you?" I asked. Poppy and Sweetie looked like they had been spit out by the lawn mower.

Sugar came running across the yard with the hose.

"WE'RE COMING FOR YOU, MOM!! WE WON'T LET THE ALIENS TAKE YOU!"

She aimed the hose directly at the front of the giant, round barbecue. The water came out fast and hard and quickly knocked it over.

"GIVE ME BACK MY MOTHER, YOU CHICKEN-STEALING ALIENS!"

The back door swung open with a giant squeak.

The chicks all lay down flat in the grass. Excellent camouflage, I noticed. I hightailed it out of there. Dumb squirrel was standing right in the middle of it all, frozen. Poor kid stuck out like a . . . dumb squirrel.

Barbara ran out of the house. Her brand-new, green barbecue grill was on the ground, surrounded by hot dogs and smoking charcoal.

"You pesky squirrel!" she hollered. "Get out of here!!"

She picked up the hose, gave Tail a good spray. The water exposed the chicks in the grass, too, but Barbara was too distracted by the small fire that was threatening her potted begonias.

Chapter 10

As soon as Barbara's back was turned, I tossed the Chicken Squad and a couple of hot dogs into the shoe and carried it back to the coop. The dumb, wet squirrel was right behind us.

"Hot dogs!" said Sugar. "Of course! The aliens weren't here for chickens, they were after the hot dogs!"

"Everybody loves hot dogs," said Poppy. "But I'm not sure a hot dog would make a very good pet."

"It's food, Poppy," said Sugar. "The aliens were after food. Good thing we stopped them. Look how many they stole! They filled up their whole space-ship with hot dogs!"

Sugar tossed one to the wet squirrel. "Thanks for your help, Tail!"

"What happens to the aliens now?" asked Tail.

"Their ship is down for good. They'll send another one. Invisible, next time, to avoid our detection. They'll rescue their friends and take off. They won't be back. Not after what we did to them. You're safe, kid. We're all safe now."

"And we thought they were here

for us." Poppy laughed. "Like anybody would eat a chicken!"

"They *are* from outer space," said Sugar. "Who knows what kind of crazy stuff they eat out there."

"What's with the shoe?" I asked.

"There was nobody left to watch it," said Poppy.

"I licked it and rolled it," said Sweetie proudly. "Just like Sugar said."

"Ew," said Tail.

"Excellent work, Sweetie," said Dirt.

Moosh walked into the chicken coop with fresh flowers from her garden. The Chicken Squad surrounded her with a BIG, ENORMOUS, and

HUGE Chicken Squad hug.

"Is that the dead squirrel?" she asked, looking at Tail.

"No," said Tail. "I'm the *brave* squirrel."

"You sure are, kid," said Sugar. "You sure are."

Epilogue

I know what you're thinking. You're thinking, J. J., you've traveled the world, seen it all, don't you know a barbecue when you see one? Sure, kid, I know a barbecue. Every dog knows a barbecue. Best smell in the world. But why tell the Chicken Squad? They're always looking for something to do. It keeps 'em out of my hair, plus, Tail finally learned his shapes. See? Everybody wins when you let them find their own way.

And let's not mention the eating-chicken thing, okay? They may act tough, but I don't think they'd take it very well.

shoe!

Doreen Cronin is the author of many *New York Times*–bestselling picture books, including the Caldecott Honor Book *Click, Clack, Moo: Cows That Type* and most recently, *Click, Clack, Boo!* Her hobbies include lurking in the shadows and solving imaginary crimes. She lives in Brooklyn, New York, where she keeps her fedora collection behind lock and key.

Kevin Cornell draws from his intergalactic command base located in Philadelphia, Pennsylvania. Some of his most successful Earth missions include illustrating *Mustache!* and *Count the Monkeys* by Mac Barnett, *Lulu's Mysterious Mission* by Judith Viorst, and *The Trouble with Chickens* by Doreen Cronin. Make first contact with him at kevskinrug.com!